DIEGO'S ARCTIC RESCUE

adapted by Erica David
based on the screenplay written by Chris Gifford
illustrated by Art Mawhinney

Simon Spotlight/Nickelodeon
New York London Toronto Sydney

Based on the TV series *Go, Diego, Go!*™ as seen on Nick Jr.®

SIMON SPOTLIGHT
An imprint of Simon & Schuster Children's Publishing Division
1230 Avenue of the Americas, New York, New York 10020
© 2009 Viacom International Inc. All rights reserved.
NICK JR., *Go, Diego, Go!*, and all related titles, logos, and characters are trademarks of Viacom International Inc.
All rights reserved, including the right of reproduction in whole or in part in any form.
SIMON SPOTLIGHT and colophon are registered trademarks of Simon & Schuster, Inc.
Manufactured in the United States of America
First Edition
2 4 6 8 10 9 7 5 3 1
ISBN: 978-1-4169-8504-4

It was a cold and windy day at the top of the world. Diego and his friend Baby Jaguar were studying polar bears at the Arctic Animal Refuge near the North Pole.

"Polar bears are cool!" Baby Jaguar exclaimed.

"They sure are," Diego replied.

"There are polar bears inside these large snow mounds. We can see them if we use my infrared binoculars," Diego explained.

Diego and Baby Jaguar used the binoculars to look inside of the snow mounds. They saw a mommy polar bear and her two babies. The baby polar bears were excited to get out to play. They quickly dug through the snow mound to reach the outside.

Once outside, the baby polar bears began to run and jump and play. The mommy polar bear watched them proudly.

Diego and Baby Jaguar watched as the polar bears walked to the water.

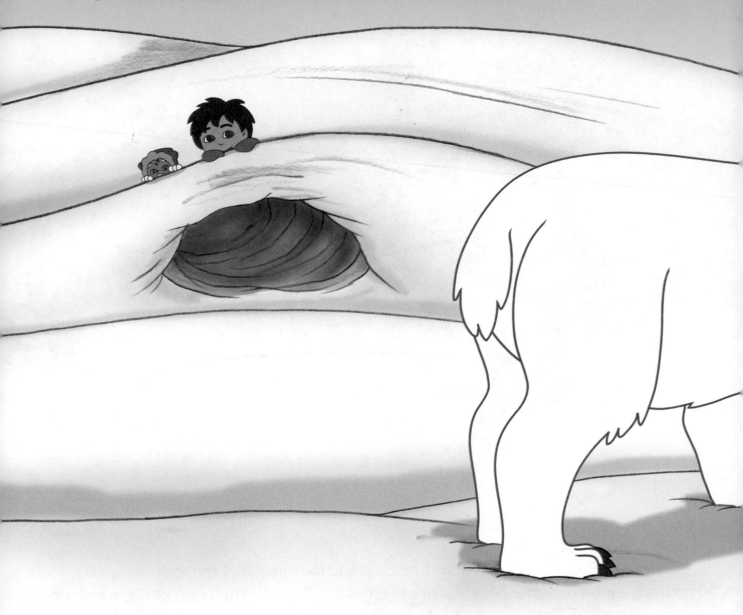

"What are they looking for, Diego?" Baby Jaguar asked.

"Ice floes," Diego answered. "Polar bears need to stand on ice floes to fish for their food in the ocean."

The mommy polar bear and her cubs jumped onto the ice floes.
"Boy, those polar bears are good jumpers!" Baby Jaguar said.
The polar bears quickly caught their food and began to eat.
Suddenly everyone heard a voice calling for help.

"There's an animal way out there, Diego!" Baby Jaguar said.

"My Spotting Scope can help me see what kind of animal's in trouble," Diego explained. He pulled out his Spotting Scope and scanned the waves. "It's a polar bear!"

"I need something to help me rescue the polar bear," Diego said.

"Rescue Pack can help," said Baby Jaguar.

"Yeah, Rescue Pack can transform into anything I need! *¡Actívate!*" said Diego. Rescue Pack transformed into a water scooter and Diego rode it out to help the polar bear.

Diego stopped alongside the polar bear and tossed her a life preserver. The bear grabbed on and Diego towed her back to shore behind his water scooter.

"You must be tired, polar bear," Diego said once they reached the shore.

"Diego, you have to help me! My babies are on an island far away. I went out swimming to find food for them, but the ice floes melted. I swam too far and couldn't get back," the mommy polar bear explained.

"Don't worry, Mommy Polar Bear. I can get your babies and bring them back to you," Diego said. "Click the Camera will help me find them."

Diego took Click the Camera from his pocket. Click zoomed through the Arctic with her lens. At last she located the baby polar bears on a small island and snapped a photo.

"My babies! My babies!" said the mommy polar bear as she looked at the photo. "It's okay, Mommy Polar Bear, I'm on my way to find them!" Diego said. "Baby Jaguar, you stay here and help the nice mommy polar bear while I look for her cubs." "Good luck getting the baby polar bears. I know you can do it!" Baby Jaguar said.

   Diego hopped onto his water scooter and sped out into the ocean to find the island where Click had seen the baby polar bears. After a while, his water scooter made a funny noise and began to slow down. It was losing power!

   Fortunately, Diego saw a boat in the distance. He used his Spotting Scope to get a closer look and saw that his sister, Alicia, was onboard. Diego called to her and paddled in her direction. Soon he reached the boat and Alicia helped to pull him aboard.

"¡*Gracias*, Alicia! Thank you!" Diego said. "I'm on a rescue mission and I need your help. We've got to get two baby polar bears back to their mommy."

"There's no time to waste. Let's go!" Alicia replied. She got behind the wheel of the boat and started driving.

Diego looked out across the water. "Alicia, how much longer until we get to the island?" he asked.

"It should be on the other side of this narrow water path," she answered.

Diego looked at the water path.

"Uh-oh, Alicia! The path is too small for the boat to fit through," he said.

"Let's use the rescue computer to find an animal that can give us a ride," Alicia suggested.

The rescue computer showed three animals close enough to help them: an arctic fish, a blue whale, and a beluga whale. Alicia and Diego thought like scientists. The fish was small enough to fit through the water path, but was too small to carry them. The blue whale was large enough to carry them, but too large to fit through the path. At last they found the animal that was just right. The beluga whale was large enough to carry them *and* small enough to fit through the water path.

Diego and Alicia asked the beluga whale for a ride. He happily agreed to carry them.

The beluga whale carried Alicia and Diego into the water path on his back. Just then, they spotted a line of walruses up ahead. They were blocking the way!

"What should we do?" Alicia asked.

"Whales are really good jumpers," Diego explained. "Maybe we can jump over the walruses."

Diego and Alicia waited as the beluga whale swam closer and closer to the walruses. Then, when he was only a few feet away, they cried: "¡Salta! Jump, Mr. Whale!"

The beluga whale jumped into the air and sailed over the line of walruses.

A short while later the beluga whale carried Diego and Alicia safely to the shore of the island. They thanked him for the ride and set off to look for the baby polar bears. Soon they found them huddled in a cave.

"*¡Hola!* I'm Diego and this is my sister, Alicia. We're here to rescue you and bring you to your mommy," Diego explained.

"We miss our mommy!" said the baby polar bears.

"Don't worry. She's in a place with lots of snow, ice, and food. We'll take you there," Diego said.

Diego and Alicia led the baby polar bears back to the shore.

"Uh-oh, Diego! The whale is gone," Alicia said. "We'll have to find another way back to the animal refuge."

Suddenly they heard a noise. "Diego, do you hear that?" Alicia asked.

"It sounds like a helicopter," Diego replied.

"And look who's inside. It's Dora!" Alicia exclaimed.

Diego's cousin, Dora the Explorer, flew in closer to meet them. When Diego explained their mission, she agreed to give them a ride back to the animal refuge. Soon they were flying through the skies.

After a while the sky began to darken and the wind picked up. A storm was coming! The wind blew the helicopter around and around.

"We have to get out of this wind!" Dora cried. "Let's tell the helicopter to go down. *¡Baja, Helicóptero!* Down, Helicopter!"

The helicopter flew lower and lower until finally it landed with a *whoosh*! Diego, Alicia, Dora, and the baby polar bears tumbled out of the helicopter. The storm was growing stronger, so they decided to take cover in a nearby cave.

"It sure is cold in here," said Dora.

"I'll say," Diego agreed.

"Hug! Hug!" said the baby polar bears.

"The polar bears want to hug us to keep us warm," Alicia explained.

"That's a great idea!" Dora said.

Everyone huddled together and hugged the baby polar bears to keep warm.

Finally the wind stopped howling and the storm was over. The baby polar bears pushed the snow aside and dug out of the cave. When everyone was outside, Diego used his GPS to find the animal refuge.

"The Arctic Animal Refuge is just on the other side of the tallest mountain," Diego said.

"How will we get over that mountain, Diego?" Alicia asked.

"Don't worry. *Helicóptero* can transform into a snow buggy to take us over the mountain. We can tell him to transform by saying *'transfórmate'*!" Dora said.

A moment later *Helicóptero* transformed into a snow buggy.

The snow buggy carried Diego, Alicia, Dora, and the baby polar bears over the tall mountain. Baby Jaguar and the mommy polar bear were waiting for them on the other side. Mommy polar bear was thrilled to see that her babies had come home safely.

"I was really worried about you," she told them. "I love you sooooo much!"

"We missed you, Mommy!" said the baby polar bears.

"Thank you for rescuing my babies," Mommy polar bear said.

"You're welcome!" Diego, Dora, and Alicia replied.

Diego was glad to have brought the polar bear family back together again. "*¡Misión complida!*" he said. "Rescue complete!"